The Last Crusader Kingdom

The Last Crusader Kingdom

Dawn of a Dynasty
in Twelfth-Century Cyprus

Helena P. Schrader

Published by Wheatmark®
2030 East Speedway Boulevard, Suite 106
Tucson, Arizona 85719 USA
www.wheatmark.com

ISBN: 978-1-62787-517-2 (paperback)
ISBN: 978-1-62787-518-9 (ebook)
LCCN: 2017946595

Contents

Cast of Characters

Historical figures are in **bold**; characters who appear twice are marked by an *; dates in italics are estimates.

House of Jerusalem

Isabella, Queen of Jerusalem, b. 1172, reigned 1190-1205

Henri de Champagne, consort of Isabella 1192-1197

Marie de Montferrat, daughter of Isabella by her second husband, Conrad de Montferrat, b. 1192, reigned 1205–1211

Marguerite, daughter of Isabella and Champagne, *b. 1194*, died before 1205

Alice, daughter of Isabella and Champagne, *b. 1195*, m. King Hugh I of Cyprus 1210, died 1246

Philippa, daughter of Isabella and Champagne, *b. 1196*

House of Lusignan

Guy de Lusignan, King of Jerusalem 1186–1190, widower of Queen Sibylla

Aimery de Lusignan, his elder brother, King of Cyprus, 1196–1205, King of Jerusalem 1197–1205

Eschiva d'Ibelin, *b. 1165*, Aimery's first wife from ca. 1173

Guy, their eldest son, *b. 1182*, died before 1205

Burgundia, their eldest daughter, *b. 1184*

Helvis, their second daughter, *b. 1186*

John (called "Aimery" to avoid confusion with John d'Ibelin), their second son, *b. 1189*, died before 1205

Hugh, youngest son of Aimery and Eschiva, b. 1195, King of Cyprus 1205–1218

House of Ibelin

Balian d'Ibelin, *b. 1149*, Baron of Ibelin 1177–1187, Baron of Caymont 1192–*1199*

Maria Comnena, his wife, *b.1154*, Queen of Jerusalem 1167–1174, mother of Queen Isabella,* d. 1217

Helvis, their eldest daughter, b. 1178, m. **Reginald de Sidon** ca *1192*

John, their eldest son, b. 1179, Constable of Jerusalem 1198, Lord of Beirut from *1202*, d. 1236

Margaret, Balian and Maria's second daughter, *b. 1181*

Philip, Balian and Maria's second son, *b. 1182*

Eschiva*, Balian's niece

Henri de Brie, Balian's nephew, son of his half-sister Ermengard, *b. 1166*

Heloise, his wife

Anseau, their eldest son, *b. 1184* (Note: Although we know Anseau de Brie was a grandson of Balian's half-sister—either Ermengard or Stephanie—we do not know his father's name. His grandfather was Anseau.)

Conan, their second son, b. 1185

Other Barons of Outremer

Richard of Camville, appointed baillie of Cyprus by Richard I

His son Richard, "Dick," squire to Guy de Lusignan

Robert of Thornham, appointed baillie of Cyprus by Richard I

Humphrey de Toron, formerly a baron in the Kingdom of Jerusalem, first husband of Isabella of Jerusalem (the marriage was annulled by a Church court headed by the Papal Legate in November 1190)

Galganus de Cheneché, adherent of King Guy at the latest from the siege of Acre 1189 onwards

His son, **Gauvain**

Reynald Barlais, a Poitevin supporter of the Lusignans

Aimery de Rivet, seneschal of Cyprus in 1197

Walter de Bethsan

Ibelin Household

Georgios, Balian's squire

Beatrice d'Auber, Maria's widowed waiting woman, a former Saracen captive

Bart, Amalric, and Joscelyn, her sons

Anne, Beatrice's niece, lady to Eschiva de Lusignan
Sir Galvin, a Scottish knight
Sir Sebastian, a Syrian Christian knight
Sir Constantine, an Edessan knight with Armenian blood
Father Angelus, Maria Zoë's confessor, tutor to the children

Greeks

Abbot Eustathios, Abbot of Antiphonitis
Brother Zotikos, a monk of Antiphonitis
Lakis, an orphan whose parents were murdered by the Franks
Andreas Katzouroubis, an apothecary
Father Andronikos, a priest
Captain Kanakes, a pirate

Italians

Carlo di Rossi, a caravansary/khan owner
Mario, his brother
Francesco Pasquali, bailli of the Pisan commune on Cyprus

Armenians

Leo, Prince (later King) of Armenia
Simon, Lord of Corycos
Ravon, his son

House of Jerusalem

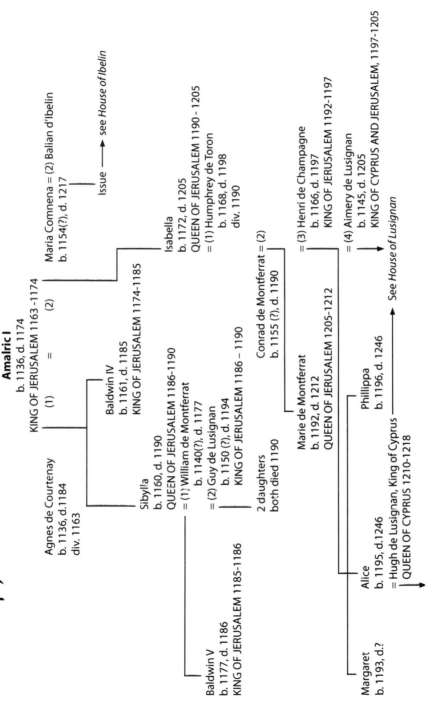

Amalric I
b. 1136, d. 1174
KING OF JERUSALEM 1163 -1174

(1) =

Agnes de Courtenay
b. 1136, d.1184
div. 1163

(2)

Maria Comnena = (2) Balian d'Ibelin
b. 1154(?), d. 1217

Issue ⟶ see *House of Ibelin*

Baldwin IV
b. 1161, d. 1185
KING OF JERUSALEM 1174-1185

Sibylla
b. 1160, d. 1190
QUEEN OF JERUSALEM 1186-1190
= (1) William de Montferrat
b. 1140(?), d. 1177
= (2) Guy de Lusignan
b. 1150 (?), d. 1194
KING OF JERUSALEM 1186 – 1190

Isabella
b. 1172, d. 1205
QUEEN OF JERUSALEM 1190 - 1205
= (1) Humphrey de Toron
b. 1168, d. 1198
div. 1190

Conrad de Montferrat = (2)
b. 1155 (?), d. 1190

= (3) Henri de Champagne
b. 1166, d. 1197
KING OF JERUSALEM 1192-1197

= (4) Aimery de Lusignan
b. 1145, d. 1205
KING OF CYPRUS AND JERUSALEM, 1197-1205

Baldwin V
b. 1177, d. 1186
KING OF JERUSALEM 1185-1186

2 daughters
both died 1190

Marie de Montferrat
b. 1192, d. 1212
QUEEN OF JERUSALEM 1205-1212

Phillippa
b. 1196, d. 1246

See *House of Lusignan* ⟶

Alice
b. 1195, d.1246
= Hugh de Lusignan, King of Cyprus
QUEEN OF CYPRUS 1210-1218 ⟶

Margaret
b. 1193, d.?

House of Lusignan

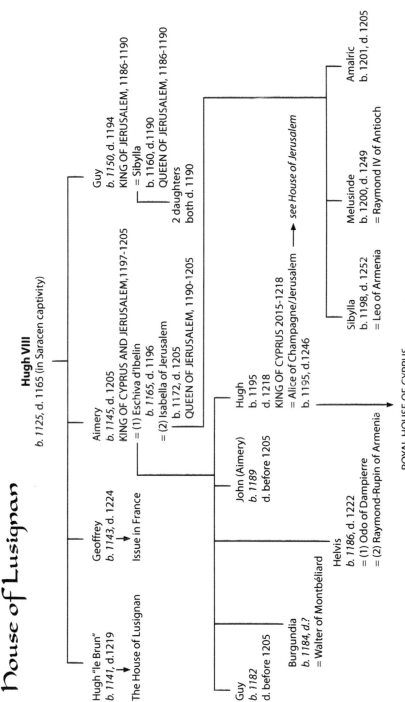

The House of Ibelin
in the 12th Century

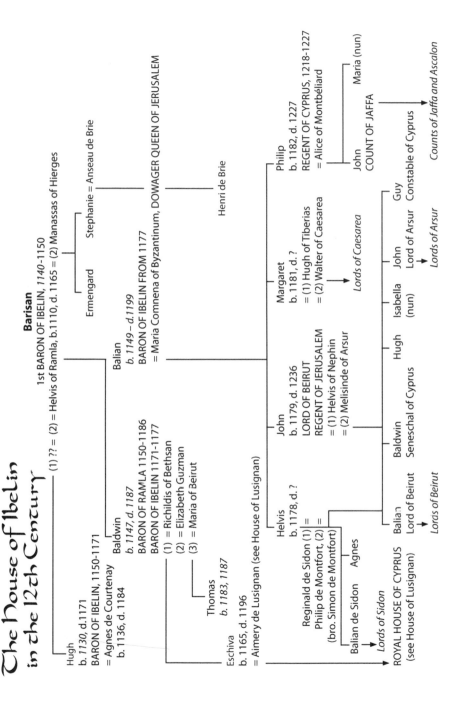

Barisan
1st BARON OF IBELIN, *1140-1150*
(1) ?? = (2) = Helvis of Ramla, b.1110, d. 1165 = (2) Manassas of Hierges

Hugh
b. *1130, d.1171*
BARON OF IBELIN, 1150-1171
= Agnes de Courtenay

Baldwin
b. 1136, d. 1184

Baldwin
b. *1147, d. 1187*
BARON OF RAMLA 1150-1186
BARON OF IBELIN 1171-1177

(1) = Richildis of Bethsan
(2) = Elizabeth Guzman
(3) = Maria of Beirut

Thomas
b. 1183, 1187

Eschiva
b. 1165, d. 1196
= Aimery de Lusignan (see House of Lusignan)

Ermengard

Stephanie = Anseau de Brie

Balian
b. 1149 – d.1199
BARON OF IBELIN FROM 1177
= Maria Comnena of Byzantinum, DOWAGER QUEEN OF JERUSALEM

Henri de Brie

Helvis
b. 1178, d. ?

Reginald de Sidon (1) =
Philip de Montfort, (2) =
(bro. Simon de Montfort)

Balian de Sidon   Agnes

Lords of Sidon

John
b. 1179, d. 1236
LORD OF BEIRUT
REGENT OF JERUSALEM
= (1) Helvis of Nephin
= (2) Melisinde of Arsur

Balian
Lord of Beirut

Lords of Beirut

Baldwin
Seneschal of Cyprus

Hugh

Isabella
(nun)

Margaret
b. 1181, d. ?
= (1) Hugh of Tiberias
= (2) Walter of Caesarea

Lords of Caesarea

John
Lord of Arsur

Lords of Arsur

Guy
Constable of Cyprus

Philip
b. 1182, d. 1227
REGENT OF CYPRUS, 1218-1227
= Alice of Montbéliard

John
COUNT OF JAFFA

Maria (nun)

Counts of Jaffa and Ascalon

ROYAL HOUSE OF CYPRUS
(see House of Lusignan)

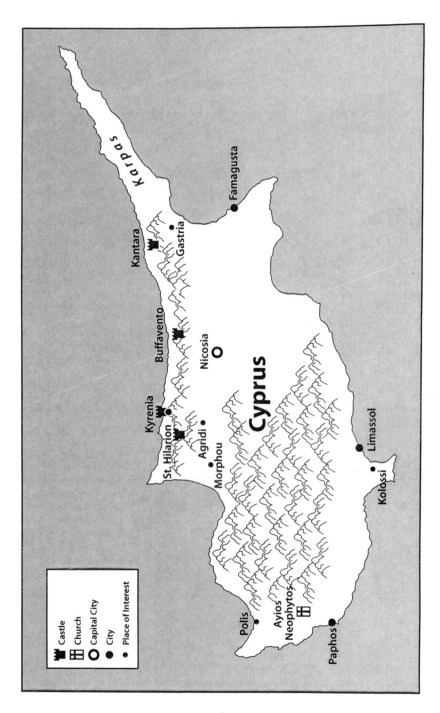

Map of Cyprus

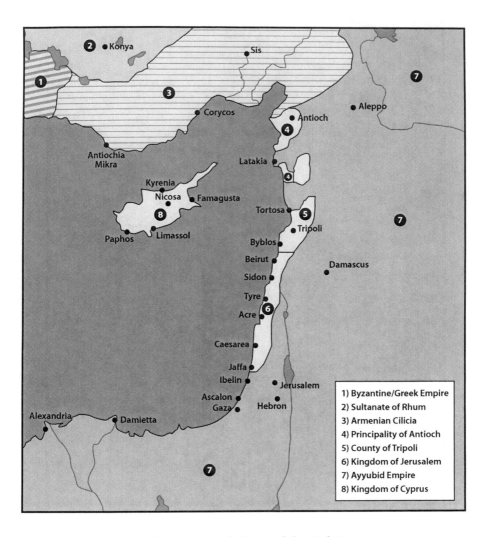

Map of Outremer at the Start of the 13th Century

1) Byzantine/Greek Empire
2) Sultanate of Rhum
3) Armenian Cilicia
4) Principality of Antioch
5) County of Tripoli
6) Kingdom of Jerusalem
7) Ayyubid Empire
8) Kingdom of Cyprus

Introduction and Acknowledgments

IN CONTRAST TO MY JERUSALEM TRILOGY,** the historical basis for this novel is very thin. The early history of the Kingdom of Cyprus is largely lost in the mists of time, and much of what we think we know—or what is currently accepted in academic circles—is dubious. There are grounds for questioning some of the common assumptions—such as the year of Balian d'Ibelin's death, the uncompromising nature of Ibelin hostility to Aimery de Lusignan, the "late" arrival of the Ibelins on Cyprus, and more. I hope to publish a history of the Ibelins, in which I will raise a number of these issues in a nonfictional format in order to invite scholarly discussion.

Meanwhile, however, this novel offers a fictional depiction of events as I believe they *could* have happened, including the usual advantages historical fiction offers with respect to exploring human nature and relationships. As a novel, this book looks at the founding of the Kingdom of Cyprus in the years 1193-1198—but also at the ever-recurring need to pacify countries or regions that have been torn apart by wars, invasions, and tyrannical government. This is a novel of medieval Cyprus—and of post-conflict reconstruction around the world in any age.

But first a few words about the period and characters in this novel, and about the major revisionist thesis incorporated in the novel and why.

We know that Richard I of England, having conquered Cyprus in May

---

** *Knight of Jerusalem, Defender of Jerusalem,* and *Envoy of Jerusalem,* published by Wheatmark in 2014, 2015, and 2016 respectively.

sold it to the Knights Templar for one hundred thousand bezants in July ~~1e~~ same year. According to Peter Edbury, the leading modern historian of ~~:dieval~~ Cyprus, Templar rule was "rapacious and unpopular," resulting in a ~~evolt~~ in April 1192. Although a Templar sortie temporarily scattered the rebels, the causes of the revolt were hardly addressed, and the latent threat of continued and renewed violence was clear. In the circumstances, the Grand Master of the Templars recognized that his Order would have to invest considerable manpower to regain control of the island. He also recognized that he did not have the resources to fight in *both* Cyprus and Syria. In consequence, he gave precedence (as he must) to the struggle on the mainland, the Holy Land itself, against the Saracens. The Templars duly returned the island to Richard of England.

Richard promptly sold the island a second time, this time to Guy de Lusignan. Guy de Lusignan had been crowned and anointed King of Jerusalem in 1186 in a coup d'état engineered by his wife, Sibylla. Although Guy de Lusignan was widely viewed as a usurper, the bulk of the barons submitted to his rule in order to fight united against the much superior forces of Saladin that threatened the Kingdom. Guy, however, proceeded to prove the low opinion of his barons correct by promptly leading the entire Christian army to an avoidable defeat on the Horns of Hattin on July 4, 1187. He spent roughly a year in Saracen captivity, while his Kingdom fell city by city and castle by castle to Saladin, until only the city of Tyre remained. Needless to say, this further discredited him with the surviving barons, prelates, and burghers of his kingdom. His claim to the crown of Jerusalem was undermined fatally when his wife, through whom he had gained it, died in November 1190. Although Guy continued to style himself "King of Jerusalem," a fiction at first bolstered by King Richard of England's support, by April 1192 King Richard had given up on him. Bowing to the High Court of Jerusalem, Richard abandoned Guy and acknowledged Conrad de Montferrat as King of Jerusalem. The sale of Cyprus to Guy was, therefore, a means of compensating him for the loss of his kingdom of Jerusalem.

Guy may have left for Cyprus at once, in which case he would have arrived in April 1192. However, this is far from certain. At that time the Third Crusade was ongoing, and it is unlikely that Guy would have been able to convince many knights to accompany him as long as Richard the Lionheart was fighting for Jerusalem and Jaffa. A more likely date for Guy's arrival on Cyprus is therefore October 1192, after Richard's departure for the West.

Guy was apparently accompanied by a small group of Frankish lords and knights whose lands had been lost to Saladin in 1187 and 1188 and had not been recaptured in the course of the Third Crusade. The names of only a few are

known. These include Humphrey de Toron, Renier de Jubail, Reynald Bâ
Walter de Bethsan, and Galganus de Cheneché. (Guy's older brother Aimery
Lusignan was notably absent.) Guy would have arrived on an island that w
either still in a state of open rebellion or completely lawless.

Admittedly, historian George Hill (who was actually an expert in ancient
history, coins, and iconography rather than a medievalist), tries to explain how
Guy arrived on an island eagerly awaiting him by inventing (that is the only
word one can use, since he cites no source) the story that the Templars "slew the
Greeks indiscriminately like sheep; a number of Greeks who sought asylum in a
church were massacred; the mounted Templars rode through [Nicosia] spitting
on their lances everyone they could reach; the streets ran with blood . . . The
Templars rode through the land, sacking villages and spreading desolation, for
the population of both cities and villages fled to the mountains." (George Hill,
A History of Cyprus, Volume 2: The Frankish Period 1192 – 1432," Cambridge
University Press, 1948, p. 37.)

There's a serious problem with this lurid tale. As Hill himself admits, the
Templars had just fourteen knights on Cyprus and twenty-nine sergeants, while
Edbury calculates that the Greek population of the island was roughly one
hundred thousand. Yes, in a surprise sortie to fight their way out of Nicosia and
flee to Acre (as we know they did) the Templars probably killed many civilians,
including innocent ones. It is unlikely that the fleeing Templars would have
taken the time to stop and slaughter people collected in a church, however,
because that would have given the armed insurgents (who had forced them to
seek refuge in their commandery in the first place) an opportunity to rally. They
certainly did not have the time and resources to massacre people in other cities
scattered over nearly ten thousand square kilometers of island. In short, we can
be sure the Templars killed enough people to be remembered with hatred, but
not enough to break the resistance to Latin rule, much less to denude the island
of its population. If nothing else, if they had broken the resistance, they would
not have fled to Acre, admitted defeat, and urged the Grand Chapter to return
Cyprus to Richard of England!

Despite the absurdity of the notion that Guy arrived on a peaceful island
willing to receive him without resistance, most histories today repeat a charming
story that as soon as Guy arrived on Cyprus, he sent to his arch-enemy Saladin
for advice on how to rule it. What is more, the ever-chivalrous and wise Sultan
graciously responded that "if he wants the island to be secure, he must give it
all away." (See Edbury, *The Kingdom of Cyprus and the Crusades, 1191 – 1374,*
Cambridge University Press, 1991, p. 16.) Allegedly, based on this advice, Guy

ted settlers from all the Christian countries of the eastern Mediterranean to tle on Cyprus, offering everyone rich rewards and making them marry the ocal women. According to this fairy tale, the dispossessed people of Syria, both high and low, flooded to Cyprus and were rewarded with rich fiefs, until Guy had only enough land to support just twenty household knights—but after that everyone lived happily ever after.

History isn't like that, although—often—there is a kernel of truth in such legends. I think it is fair to assume that many of the men and women who had lost their lands and livelihoods to the Saracens after Hattin did *eventually* come to settle on Cyprus, but I question that they arrived in the first two years after Guy acquired the island. The reason I doubt this is simple. The Knights Templar had just abandoned the island because it would *be too costly, time-consuming, and difficult to pacify*. In short, whoever came to Cyprus with Guy in early or late 1192 would *not* have found an empty island—much less one full of happy natives waiting to welcome them with song and flowers. On the contrary, the natives were *already* in active rebellion against the Templars and ready to resist further attempts by the Latins to control and dominate them. Perhaps the one sentence about making the settlers marry local women is a hint to a more chilling reality: that *years* of resistance to Latin rule left the local population with few young men, but many widows, by the time the settlers finally flooded in.

Furthermore, we know that at no time in his life did Guy de Lusignan distinguish himself by wisdom or common sense. He alienated his brother-in-law King Baldwin IV and nearly the entire High Court of Jerusalem within just three years of his marriage to Sibylla. He lost his entire kingdom in a disastrous and unnecessary campaign less than a year after he was crowned king. He started a strategically nonsensical siege of Acre that consumed crusader lives and resources for three years. He did nothing of note the entire time Richard the Lionheart was in the Holy Land. Is it really credible that he then took control of a rebellious island (that the Templars thought beyond their capacity to pacify) and set everything right in less than two years?

I think not. And Guy *had* only two years, because he died in 1194, either in April/May or toward the end of the year, depending on which source one consults. That is too little time even for a more competent leader to be the architect of Cyprus' success. That honor belongs, I believe, to Guy's older brother, the ever-competent Aimery de Lusignan, who was Lord of Cyprus not two years, but eleven.

It was certainly Aimery who obtained a crown by submitting the island to the Holy Roman Emperor, and it was Aimery who established a Latin Church hierarchy on the island. Indeed, there is ample evidence of Aimery's able admin-

istration of Cyprus and, from 1197 to 1205, of the Kingdom of Jeru.
well. It was Aimery de Lusignan who collected the oral tradition for th
of Jerusalem (which had worked so well) and had them written down in a
codex known as *The Book of the King*. Thus it was Aimery who not only founc
the dynasty that would last three hundred years, but also laid the legal and instr
tutional foundations that would serve Cyprus so well into the fifteenth century.
It is therefore far more likely that it was Aimery, not Guy, who brought settlers
in—after first pacifying the Greek population and institutionalizing tolerance
for all natives irrespective of religion or language that mirrored the customs of
the Kingdom of Jerusalem. It is this thesis that forms the basis of this novel.

There is, however, another "mystery" that I seek to explain in this novel—
namely, the roots of Ibelin influence on Cyprus. Historians such as Edbury
posit that the Ibelins were inveterate opponents of the Lusignans until the early
thirteenth century. They note that there is no *record* of Ibelins setting foot on the
island of Cyprus before 1210, and insist that it is "certain" they were not among
the early settlers—while admitting that it is *impossible* to draw up a complete list
of the early settlers. Edbury, furthermore, admits that "it is not possible to trace
[the Ibelins'] rise in detail," yet argues it was based on close ties to King Hugh I.
Close? Hugh was the son of a cousin, which in my opinion does not constitute
terribly "close" kinship.

Even more difficult to understand in the conventional version of events is
that the Ibelins became *so* powerful and entrenched within just eight years of
their supposed "first appearance" on Cyprus, when an Ibelin, presumably with
the consent of the Cypriot High Court (that is, the barons and bishops of the
island, who had supposedly been on the island far longer), was appointed regent
of Cyprus. A decade later, these alleged "latecomers" to Cyprus led a successful
baronial rebellion against the most powerful monarch in Christendom—the
Holy Roman Emperor Friedrich II—and all without, allegedly, holding fiefs on
Cyprus. I don't think that's credible.

My thesis and the basis of this novel is this: while the Ibelin brothers Baldwin
and Balian d'Ibelin were inveterate opponents of *Guy* de Lusignan, they were on
friendly terms with *Aimery* de Lusignan. Aimery was, for a start, married to an
Ibelin: Baldwin's daughter and Balian's niece! We have references, furthermore,
to them "supporting" Aimery as late as Saladin's invasion of 1183. I think the
Ibelins were very capable of distinguishing between the two Lusignan brothers,
and of judging Aimery by his own strengths rather than condemning him for
his brother's weaknesses.

Furthermore, the conventional argument is that Balian d'Ibelin died in late
1193 because he disappears from the charters of the Kingdom of Jerusalem at

ate. While this is a reasonable argument, it is not compelling. The fact Balian d'Ibelin disappears from the records of the Kingdom of Jerusalem 1193 *may* mean that he died, but it could just as easily mean that he was ccupied elsewhere. For example, he could have been busy on Cyprus.

The lack of documentary proof for his *presence* on Cyprus is not grounds for dismissing this possibility, because 1) the Kingdom of Cyprus did not yet exist, so there was no chancery and no elaborate system for keeping records, writs, charters, and so on, and 2) those who would soon make Cyprus a kingdom were probably busy fighting a hundred thousand outraged Orthodox Greeks on the island!

But why would Balian d'Ibelin go to Cyprus at this time if it was such a wild and dangerous place?

Because his wife, Maria Comnena, was a Byzantine princess, related to the last Greek ruler of the island, Isaac Comnenus. She spoke Greek, understood the mentality of the population, and probably had good ties (or could forge them) to the Greek Orthodox elites, secular and ecclesiastical, on the island. She had the means to help Aimery pacify his unruly realm. Furthermore, Balian was a proven diplomat par excellence, who would also have been a great asset to Aimery.

If one accepts that Guy de Lusignan failed to pacify the island in his short time as lord, then what would have been more natural than for his successor Aimery to appeal to his wife's kin to help him get a grip on his unruly inheritance?

If Balian d'Ibelin and Maria Comnena played a role in helping Aimery establish his authority on Cyprus, it is nearly certain they would have been richly rewarded with lands and fiefs on the island once the situation settled down. Such feudal holdings would have given the Ibelins a seat on the High Court of Cyprus, which would explain their influence on it. Furthermore, these Cypriot estates would most likely have fallen to their younger son, Philip, because their firstborn son, John, was heir to their holdings in the Kingdom of Jerusalem. John was first Constable of the Kingdom of Jerusalem, then Lord of the hugely important barony and port of Beirut, and finally, after King Aimery's death, regent of the Kingdom of Jerusalem for his half-sister's daughter. Philip, on the other hand, was Constable of *Cyprus* and later regent of Cyprus for Henri I—despite the fact that his elder brother was still alive at the time.

Last but not least, no historian is able to explain why Aimery de Lusignan named John d'Ibelin Constable of Jerusalem in 1198, when John was just eighteen or at most nineteen years old. It has been suggested that the appointment was "just nominal" and didn't carry real authority—but there is no evidence of this. To the contrary, the position was anything but nominal throughout the preceding century. Furthermore, even if nominal, why would Aimery appoint the young Ibelin to such a prestigious and lucrative post if Ibelins and Lusignans

were still, as historians insist, bitter enemies? Postulating a personal
between Aimery and John, on the other hand, would explain it. Given
differences, the relationship of lord and squire is the most plausible explan
The lord/squire relationship brought men very close and gave each great ins
into the personality, strengths, and weaknesses of the other. It was also comme
for youths to serve a relative, and so quite logical for John to serve his cousin's
husband.

While this is all speculation, it is reasonable and does not contradict what
is in the historical record. It is only in conflict with what modern historians
have postulated based on a paucity of records. I hope, therefore, that readers
will enjoy following me down this speculative road as I explore what *might* have
happened in these critical years at the close of the twelfth century.

For readers familiar with the Jerusalem Trilogy, there is one major and one
minor change. First, whereas I found it expedient to invent a younger brother
for Balian in the form of "Henri d'Ibelin" for the Jerusalem Trilogy, further
research has uncovered a very real nephew who would better serve the purposes
of the narrative in this (and coming) books. "Henri d'Ibelin" has, therefore,
been transformed into "Henri de Brie," the son of Balian's half-sister. Second,
I changed the name of Balian's older brother from Baldwin to Barisan "Barry"
to avoid confusion with King Baldwin, who was a major character in the first
two books of the trilogy. In this and subsequent books, I will refer to Balian's
older brother by his correct name, Baldwin. For other minor changes, see the
historical notes.

I would like to take this opportunity to thank my editor Christina Dickson
for her meticulous editing and overall support and encouragement. I'd like to
thank my cover designer Mikhail Greuli for a lovely cover that captures the
beauty of Cyprus and the juxtaposition of Orthodox Church and invading
Franks. Last but not least, I wish to thank all my test readers for their candid but
constructive criticism. All of these people contributed to making this a better
book, which I hope you, as readers, will enjoy. If you do, please write a review
and post it on Amazon and/or Goodreads. Thank you all!

Prologue: Lusignan's Wolves
Antiphonitis Monastery, Cyprus
March 1193

BROTHER ZOTIKOS WAS WORRIED ABOUT THE monastery's cow. They had only one at the moment, because the older cow had died during the winter. The surviving cow was with calf, and she had been restless all afternoon. So when the other eight monks retired to the dormitory after vespers, Brother Zotikos went out to the barn. The fieldstone structure sat farther down the steep slope from the church, crouching against the eastern wall of the complex, so Zotikos took a brass oil lamp to light his way. He set the lamp carefully on the flagstone porch to the barn. (Too many fires had been caused by knocked-over lamps in barns . . .) Just as he was about to step inside, he heard a noise beyond the wall that made him freeze.

"Help!" someone called in a faint, breathless, but desperate voice. "Help!"

Brother Zotikos was in his early twenties, of burly build and robust health. He had joined the monastery two years earlier, but before that he had helped his father in their cooperage. He didn't hesitate a moment. He ran to open the gate that gave access to the rugged track leading down to the main road from Kyrenia to Karpasia.

The gate was barred by a heavy timber beam, but Brother Zotikos lifted this clear of the supports and opened the gate. The youth who had been leaning against it fell inside, collapsing to the ground at his feet. "Help!" he repeated.

Brother Zotikos bent over him. The youth looked healthy, but he was y able to speak for breathing so heavily. He had apparently run up the steep from the coastal road. "They're slaughtering us!" he gasped out, dragging ..mself upright by grasping Brother Zotikos' legs and black cassock. "My dad— ne sent me—to fetch—help!"

"Who is slaughtering you?" Brother Zotikos asked as he helped the youth up. He recognized him as Lakis, the younger son of the miller at the foot of the gorge.

"Franks! Lusignan's wolves!"

"But why? That's—" Brother Zotikos cut himself off. What was the point of protesting or questioning? The youth was clearly terrified, and something had to be happening to make him so. But they were just four servants, two shepherds, nine monks, and the abbot. Furthermore, except for himself and Brother Athanasios, the monks and servants were elderly, not to say feeble.

Lakis misunderstood his hesitation and gasped out: "They set fire to the oil press! If you don't believe me, come and see!"

Yanking hard on Brother Zotikos' hand, Lakis pulled him out of the walled compound and along the stony path that zigzagged steeply down the slope. At the first bend, a view opened up of the gorge falling sharply northeast to the fishing village that sat below the monastery on the coast. Brother Zotikos gasped. It wasn't just one building that was on fire, but a half-dozen. The smell of smoke was in the air and his hair stood up on the back of his neck as a faint, high-pitched scream reached him on the breeze. It was a woman's scream, and it made his blood run cold.

By morning, more than two dozen villagers had reached the refuge of the monastery. They arrived breathless, with scratched and bleeding legs from cutting through the underbrush, and many of them were still barefoot or in their nightclothes. They had not had time to grab anything but their wives and children. The dazed women sat clutching their screaming infants, who had long since soaked their diapers and wet the clothes of their mothers as well. The smaller children clustered around them, too frightened and bewildered to even cry. The men argued and ranted, outdoing one another with the tales of horror they had witnessed.

Father Eustathios listened to them patiently without comment. Then he ordered the elder monks to see that the visitors were given food, a chance to wash themselves and their clothes, and a place to sleep. Finally, he told Athanasios and Zotikos to accompany him down the hill. Father Eustathios, who was in his fifties and suffered from arthritis, rode the monastery donkey; the two young monks walked.

As they descended toward the village, they came upon sma_
lone villagers still dragging themselves up the hill to the monastery. _
men with injuries or wounds, hysterical girls carried by their brothers, _
clutching injured children. Partway down the road, they came upon a w_
and her unconscious husband. The man's head was covered in crusted and _
shimmering blood. His wife poured out a tale of horror with a flood of tears. H_
elder son and husband had tried to stop the Franks from taking her daughter
from the house, but they had smashed her boy's face with a mace, killing him
with a single blow, and everyone could see the state her husband was in! As for
her daughter . . .

When they approached the mill that lay a little outside of town, they first
encountered a terrified mule that had evidently broken free of its stall at the
price of tearing its shoulder open. A hundred yards further, they found only
the charred ruins of the mill itself, including the partially incinerated corpses of
Lakis' parents and siblings.

After that it just got worse.

It took them two days to bury all the victims. The survivors helped the
monks, and even started to scratch together what was left of their lives. Lakis was
told he could stay at the monastery, helping with the livestock, until someone
could get word to his maternal uncle in Karpasia that he was orphaned.

But once the last Mass had been said and the last of their guests (save Lakis)
had departed, Brother Zotikos realized that he could not just accept what had
happened. Innocent people had been slaughtered while they peacefully pursued
their humble lives. Pious and devout women had been defiled in a church—
before being butchered. Men had been murdered for defending their homes,
their livelihoods, and their daughters.

How could they just go back to praising God as if nothing had happened?
Why should he *praise* God at all? For what? For letting this happen?

Brother Zotikos' blood was boiling. He could neither sleep nor pray for
fury. His rage was too great, and it kept growing. Who were these men who
had worked such destruction? What right did they have to destroy the lives of
others? Why were they allowed to break the laws of civilization and Christianity
with impunity?

When his rage had built up to the point that he could contain it no longer,
Brother Zotikos burst in on his abbot and exploded. "We can't just suffer this!
We can't—shouldn't—'turn the other cheek'! They are monsters! Worse than
Saracens! We must fight them!"

Father Eustathios was hunched over his desk reading something, and he

.ed to face his outraged subordinate. His eyes were piercing and they
⌐ Brother Zotikos, making him feel both naked and uncertain. "You
⌐ fight the Franks?" he asked coldly.

Brother Zotikos already felt a little foolish under the abbot's gaze, but he
rsisted. "Yes! We can't allow them to just slaughter us as if we were less than
sheep! Mere insects! They have treated us worse than infidels, worse than livestock! As if neither we nor they were Christians!"

"You are aware," Father Eustathios asked in a low but clear voice, "that these
Franks have just fought Saladin to a standstill?"

"That was the English King—who promised us we would be left in
peace, only to betray us by selling Cyprus first to the Templars and now to the
Lusignan!" Brother Zotikos shot back furiously. "King Richard might have been
invincible, but Lusignan lost his kingdom in a single day! He's an idiot as well
as a monster!"

"Maybe, but he is supported by a pack of greedy wolves who have lost their
lands to the Saracens and have come here to steal ours in compensation. That
makes them both greedy and desperate. Desperate, greedy men are notoriously
vicious, tenacious, and very dangerous."

"And for that reason we should just roll over and offer them our throats?"
Brother Zotikos shot back indignantly. His dark eyes burned over his thick
black beard.

"No," Father Eustathios answered, adding in a voice that was so low it was
hardly more than a hiss, "for that reason we must not bellow like a wounded
bear but remain silent as a cobra—until we strike."

Brother Zotikos felt as if he himself had just been seized by the deadly fangs
of a poisonous snake, and his eyes widened in sudden understanding. "You
mean . . . ?"

"Do you think you are the only man on Cyprus with a sense of honor? The
only Greek with spirit and courage? Don't be so presumptuous! But silence and
stealth are our best shields. We must collect our strength, and we must await the
right opportunity. When it comes—whenever it comes—we must strike without
noise or warning. We must survive to strike again and again and again—until
one by one, handful by handful, troop by troop, they are all as dead as the nuns
of Agios Kosmos."

Chapter One

Arrest of a Constable

Acre, Kingdom of Jerusalem
April 1193

THE HEAVY POUNDING OF A MAILED fist on the wooden door reverberated through the narrow stone house. The cook was startled from her sleep and grabbed her groggy husband in terror. "Christ's bones! Who can that be in the middle of the night?"

On the far side of the room by the still-smoldering fireplace, the two scullery boys sat up. "What is it? Who is it?" the boys asked one another in fright.

"Open up!" a gruff voice shouted through the door.

From the floor above came the sound of muffled voices: Lady Eschiva's voice was alarmed and questioning, Lord Aimery answered with a calming growl. Then a child started crying. Lady Eschiva hurried to the children's chamber, and Lord Aimery leaned over the railing to call down the stairs: "Answer the door! Find out who it is and what they want!"

The man-of-all-work in the little household rolled out of the box bed with a grumble and padded barefoot to the door. His hairy, unshapely legs protruded naked from beneath his shirt. "Coming! Coming!" he called as the knock was repeated urgently. When he reached the door, he turned the key and pulled back the bolt to crack it open and peer into the street.

The heavy door was shoved open into his face with so much force that it flung him against the wall and smashed his nose. Blood gushed down to his mouth, and his forehead would wear an ugly bruise.

forced their way inside were dressed in chain mail from head to foot, wore skullcap helmets with heavy nose guards. Most terrifying of all, the surcoats with the arms of Jerusalem on them: they were the King's men.

"Where's Lord Aimery?" one of them barked at the stunned servants.

"I'm here!" Aimery called from the floor above. Without hesitation the four armored men pushed past the frightened servants to the stairs at the back of the vaulted room. They pounded up to the next floor, and as they emerged out of the stairway, they found the Constable of Jerusalem hastily donning his surcoat while a young squire held his sword ready for him to take.

"Hold that, boy!" one of the King's men shouted, springing to put himself between the squire and the Constable. He pushed the squire backwards, pinned him against the wall, and wrenched the sword out of his hands with little trouble.

Meanwhile, the sergeant turned his attention to the Constable himself. "My lord, you are under arrest for high treason! Either you come with us willingly, or we have orders to take you by force."

"The charges are false and slanderous!" he told the sergeant firmly. "I will defend myself before the High Court."

Aimery de Lusignan was a handsome man in his early fifties. His shoulder-length blond hair was somewhat disheveled and his face was sprouting the beginnings of a beard, but he had managed to pull on braies, hose, and a gambeson over his nightshirt. He stood with his shoulders squared and his head held high.

"Maybe. For now you're coming with us!" the sergeant answered bluntly, ominously lowering his hand to his hilt.

"Where are you taking me?" the Constable asked gruffly.

"To the royal dungeon, where all traitors are held! Now, are you coming willingly, or must I use force?"

"Will you at least allow me to put on boots?" the Constable asked back in a voice edged with bitterness.

"No tricks!" the sergeant warned, drawing his sword for emphasis before nodding to Lord Aimery to get on with it.

The Constable walked across the room to where his knee-high boots were standing, the soft upper parts flopped over on their sides. He took the suede boots, sat on the nearest chest, and pulled them on one at a time. Then he stood and surveyed the room briefly; whether he was looking for a chance to escape or simply taking a last leave was unclear. The king's men blocked the door, their swords drawn. They not only ensured he was trapped, they also kept his wife out. He could hear her anxious voice in the hall demanding an explanation. His squire was still pinned against the far wall, his eyes wide with shock and disbelief.

"John, get word to your father of what has happened," the Constable